The Kingdom of Wrenly

of

Wrenly

=== 13 ===

The Thirteenth Knight

By Jordan Quinn

Illustrated by Robert McPhillips

LITTLE SIMON

New York   London   Toronto   Sydney   New Delhi

LITTLE SIMON

An imprint of Simon & Schuster Children's Publishing Division

1230 Avenue of the Americas, New York, New York 10020

First Little Simon paperback edition May 2018

Copyright © 2018 by Simon & Schuster, Inc.

Also available in a Little Simon hardcover edition.

All rights reserved, including the right of reproduction in whole or in part in any form.

LITTLE SIMON is a registered trademark of Simon & Schuster, Inc., and associated colophon is a trademark of Simon & Schuster, Inc.

For information about special discounts for bulk purchases, please contact Simon & Schuster Special Sales at 1-866-506-1949 or business@simonandschuster.com.

The Simon & Schuster Speakers Bureau can bring authors to your live event. For more information or to book an event contact the Simon & Schuster Speakers Bureau at 1-866-248-3049 or visit our website at www.simonspeakers.com.

Designed by Laura Roode

Manufactured in the United States of America 0418 MTN

2 4 6 8 10 9 7 5 3 1

Library of Congress Cataloging-in-Publication Data

Names: Quinn, Jordan, author. | McPhillips, Robert, 1971– illustrator.

Title: The Thirteenth Knight / by Jordan Quinn ; illustrated by Robert McPhillips.

Description: First Little Simon edition. | New York : Little Simon, 2018. | Series: The Kingdom of Wrenly ; 13 | Summary: Clara, Tublock, and many others compete to become one of the ultimate defenders of the Kingdom of Wrenly, a member of the elite Knight Spires. | Identifiers: LCCN 2017044069 | ISBN 9781534412743 (pbk) | ISBN 9781534412750 (hc) | ISBN 9781534412767 (eBook)

Subjects: | CYAC: Knights and knighthood—Fiction. | Contests—Fiction. | Conduct of life—Fiction. | Princes—Fiction. | BISAC: JUVENILE FICTION / Fantasy & Magic. | JUVENILE FICTION / Action & Adventure / General. | JUVENILE FICTION / Readers / Chapter Books.

Classification: LCC PZ7.Q31945 Thi 2018 | DDC [Fic]—dc23

LC record available at https://lccn.loc.gov/2017044069

CONTENTS

CHAPTER 1

The Horn
of the Spires

The snow-frosted peaks of Flatfrost sparkled in the midmorning sun. Prince Lucas watched his best friend, Clara, try to catch snowflakes on her tongue.

"You look ridiculous!" Lucas said, laughing.

Clara stuck her tongue out at the prince. "Who cares! I'm just glad it's cold outside!"

Back home, the palace had been suffering from a terrible heat wave. Lucas and Clara were happy to have escaped. Prince Lucas's pet dragon, on the other hand, was not. Ruskin was a red dragon and red dragons loved hot weather—the hotter the better.

In spite of hating the cold, Ruskin
made the best sled chute ever with
his fiery breath. The melted snow
had frozen into a smooth, slippery
half-pipe.

4

Lucas, Clara, and their giant friends Tublock, Thea, and Farfalee took turns slip-sliding down the chute. As they dragged their sleds back up the mountain for another run, a horn sounded.

BALOOOOO! The eerie sound wailed through the mountains and shook snow from the treetops. Deer galloped to safety. Snow bunnies and foxes leaped into their burrows and dens.

BALOOOOO! The horn moaned again.

"What was that?" cried Tublock,

looking this way and that. The horn sounded like the wail of an unhappy giant. Farfalee and Thea huddled together, their eyes wide as saucers.

Clara's eyes had also grown wide, but for a very different reason. She knew what the sound of the horn meant. She grinned at Lucas and Tublock.

"It's the Horn of the Knight Spires!" Clara said excitedly.

Farfalee covered his ears as the moan echoed again.

"What's the Horn of the Knight Spires?" Thea asked.

Clara plunked her sled into the snow to make a bench.

"Sit down," she said, "and we'll tell you the story!"

CHAPTER 2

En Garde!

"Long ago, there was little peace in the kingdom of Wrenly," Clara began. "The king, together with the Great Dragon of Crestwood, formed a sacred band of knights called the Knight Spires of Wrenly."

Lucas made a fist. "They are the greatest knights of *all* time! Instead of riding horses, they ride powerful creatures, like bears and tigers!"

Clara nodded. "That's right! And the Great Dragon of Crestwood chose only the *best* knights from across the land to be a part of the Knight Spires. Their job was to be the *ultimate* defenders of the kingdom."

Tublock sat down with a *whump*.
Clara continued, "This year the
Knight Spires will choose a thirteenth
member to add to the squadron."

Lucas leaped to his feet as if he
were the Thirteenth Knight. He
pulled a pretend sword from his hip.

"*En garde!*" he cried, waving his pretend sword at Clara.

Clara drew her own pretend sword and pointed it toward the prince. She loved to play-fight with Lucas because she *almost always* won.

Then the play-fighting began. They lunged, tumbled, rolled over in the snow, and got back on their feet. The giant children cheered wildly.

Then Lucas fell into a snowbank.
Clara pointed her pretend sword at
him.

"Okay, okay, I surrender!" Lucas
cried.

The giants clapped for Clara.

"So, can anyone become a Knight Spire?" Thea asked.

Clara brushed the snow from her coat. "No, not just anyone," she answered. "You have to win a game in order to be chosen."

Farfalee punched the air with his fists. "What's so hard about that?" he said. "Games are *fun*."

Lucas laughed knowingly. "But *this* game is very different," he said. "The contestants are usually the bravest knights in the land. They have to perform *three* very dangerous tasks. In fact, most players never make it past the first round!"

Farfalee stopped boxing the air. "That *does* sound hard," he agreed.

Then Lucas hopped to his feet. "And that's why becoming a Knight Spire of Wrenly is such an honor! There are only twelve on their team."

As the horn sounded again, Lucas waved to Ruskin and whistled for their horses. "And because this is such an important event, we must take our leave now."

Clara nodded as Ruskin flapped his wings excitedly.

The giants waved good-bye as Lucas and Clara hopped onto their saddles and slapped their reins.

"Hurry!" Clara cried. "We don't want to miss the dubbing of the Thirteenth Knight!"

CHAPTER 3

The Prophecy

Lucas and Clara galloped toward the palace gates. Colorful banners flew from the top of every wall and turret. Each one showed the family crest of someone who had come to enter the Knight Spires competition.

The children led their horses to the stables. Then they raced to the great hall, where all the competitors and their families had gathered.

Queen Tasha greeted them as they entered. All the excitement made Lucas wish he could compete.

"I would love to become a Knight Spire," he said. "Then I would be the noblest prince ever!"

Queen Tasha rested her hand on her son's shoulder. "You already *are* the noblest prince ever," she said.

Lucas rolled his eyes. "You have to say that," he said, "because you're my *mom*."

Clara laughed, then she quickly covered her mouth before the queen heard her.

Queen Tasha smiled. "But it's also true!" she said. "You're already a great swordsman, and each day you learn how to care for the people of Wrenly— just like your father."

Clara nodded. "That's right. Plus, one day you'll oversee the kingdom, *including* the Knight Spires."

Lucas blushed. The truth was that he already had perhaps one of the most important roles in the kingdom.

Queen Tasha turned her attention to Clara. "And what about you, dear Clara?" she asked. "Have you any thoughts of competing?"

Clara breathed deeply. It sounded like such an astounding idea. "Of course I'd love to," she said, "but I'm still too young."

The queen smiled. There was a twinkle in her eye. "Perhaps not," she said. "There has been a prophecy announced while you two were in Flatfrost."

Lucas and Clara both raised an eyebrow.

"What kind of prophecy?" Lucas asked.

The queen stepped back from the crowded reception, and the children followed her.

"Well," the queen answered, "the dragons of Crestwood have foretold that this year's search for a Knight Spire would require a broader range of contestants."

"Really?" Lucas questioned.

"What does it mean when they say a broader range?" Clara asked.

The queen held up her hands so she could explain. "The Knight Spires have lowered the age limit for this year's competition," she said. "This will allow more contestants to enter, just as the prophecy foretold."

Lucas grabbed Clara's shoulders. "Clara, you *have* to try out!"

A smile swept across Clara's face. "Well then, far be it from me to reject a prophecy *and* a prince's request!"

CHAPTER 4

A Case of the Jitters

The line of contestants wrapped all the way around the palace grounds—*twice!* Clara stood behind her not-so-favorite squire, Gilbert. She wanted nothing more than to ignore him, but she decided to give him a chance. *Who knows,* she thought. *Maybe he's gotten nicer.*

"Hey, Gilbert," she said casually.

"Oh, h-h-hi, Clara!" he stammered.

Gilbert sounded nervous, so Clara smiled warmly. "Don't worry," she said reassuringly. "I'm a little nervous too, but I'm also excited!"

Gilbert acted as if being nervous was the farthest thing from his mind.

"I'm not nervous," he said. "A *real* Knight Spire never gets nervous."

But Clara noticed that Gilbert now had beads of sweat on his upper lip, too, and his neck had grown red and splotchy. He was hiding his fear.

"Being nervous is a *good* thing," Clara told him. "You can't be brave without being afraid first, because then you would have nothing to be brave about."

Gilbert's jaw dropped at Clara's clever answer. At the same time, a shadow swept over both of them. Gilbert jumped at the sudden darkness. When Clara turned around, she had to cover her mouth to hide her laughter. It was Tublock. The giant cast a large shadow over them as he blocked out the sun.

"Hey, Tublock!" Clara said. "Are you here to compete?"

Tublock nodded happily. "Well, at first I came to watch," he said. "But when I heard about the prophecy, I had to sign up."

Clara bumped fists with Tublock and introduced the giant to Gilbert. Gilbert shook Tublock's hand uncertainly. Then the three contestants moved through the line until they got to the check-in desk. King Caleb and Prince Lucas greeted them.

"Hello, friends!" Lucas said, showing them where to sign in.

Clara and Gilbert bowed before the king and the prince, and then they signed the ledger. Tublock signed in too. No giant had ever entered the competition before. The king complimented him on being the first.

As the threesome approached the arena, the Horn of the Knight Spires sounded nearby. This signaled for everyone to be seated. The competition would soon begin.

A rumble came from outside the stadium. The sound grew closer and closer. Soon three knights galloped into the arena, each riding a different beast—one on a lion, another on a tiger, and the third on a bear. The one on the lion sounded the horn again.

BALOOOOO!

The Knight Spires of Wrenly had arrived.

41

CHAPTER 5

Shush!

A hush fell over the contestants. The knights' armor gleamed in the sunlight as they lined up before the king and bowed. Tublock leaned over and gently tapped Clara on the shoulder.

"Where are the rest of them?" Tublock whispered. Unfortunately, his whisper was louder than most people's regular voices, and *everyone* heard him.

"Shhh!" Clara shushed, elbowing him. But it was too late. The Spire on the lion had heard and now looked their way. Tublock's cheeks turned red. The Spire trotted over to where Clara and Tublock were sitting and stopped in front of them.

"Your friend asked a question," said the Spire, addressing Clara. "Are you able to answer it?"

Clara didn't know if she wanted to kick Tublock or simply disappear. Then she noticed Lucas in the stands, waving his arms wildly and pointing in different directions. Clara didn't know what he was trying to tell her.

Finally she looked at the Spire and shook her head. "No, brave sir, I cannot."

Then Gilbert cleared his throat loud enough for the Spire to hear.

"Perhaps *you* can answer the Head Spire's question," the Spire on the bear said.

The crowd gasped and Clara shrank down, having embarrassed herself in front of the Head Spire.

Gilbert, on the other hand, stood tall so everyone could see him.

"The Spires are never allowed to be all in one place at the same time," he said. "They have to be spread out across the kingdom to protect *all* of Wrenly."

The Head Spire nodded. "That is the correct answer," he said, then strode on his lion toward the king.

Gilbert leaned forward so Clara could see him.

"You're welcome," he said, even though Clara had not thanked him. Then he added, "But don't expect any help during the competition."

Clara clenched her fists. Sometimes Gilbert could make her *so* mad. She had to control the urge to talk back, but fortunately, she forgot her struggle when the king stood to make an announcement.

"Welcome, each and every one of you, to the Knight Spires of Wrenly Competition!" he said. "The Knight Spires are on a quest to find their true thirteenth member. Each search leads contenders to different realms of Wrenly to prove their worth. Now the time has come to reveal where you will compete."

The horn sounded, and the Head Spire stood in his stirrups.

"Brave contestants!" he called out. "Get ready, because tomorrow we sail for the island of Crestwood."

CHAPTER 6

A Pregame Show

The king's family, the three Knight Spires, and the royal court boarded a ship bound for Crestwood. The competitors sailed on a separate ship. Friends, family, and fans had to find their own way there.

When the two ships arrived, the royal family went to the grandstand that faced Crestwood's largest volcano, Mount Fireburst.

The prince could hardly sit still. He longed to talk with Clara. He hadn't seen his best friend since the day before.

"I want to wish Clara good luck!" Lucas told his parents, searching the arena for signs of his friend.

Queen Tasha plumped the pillow on her seat. "Clara knows you're rooting for her," she reassured her son. "And we are in the front row. Surely she'll be able to see you cheering."

Lucas knew his mother was right, but he still felt antsy not being able to talk to his best friend.

The prince wasn't the only one who was restless. Ruskin couldn't sit still either. That's because Crestwood was Ruskin's birthplace. Being back on the island made him want to do dragon things. He couldn't take sitting any longer, and WHOOSH. He leaped from his seat and took flight.

"Hey, come back!" Lucas commanded as he watched his dragon fly straight to the top of the volcano. But Ruskin paid no attention.

"Don't worry," the king said. "He'll return."

The crowd watched Ruskin soar.

He flew to around the rim of the
volcano. Round and round he went.
Then the young dragon plunged
into the opening. That's when Lucas
grabbed his father's leg.

"What's he *doing*?" he cried.

The king stroked his beard. "I'd say he's showing off," he said.

"And I'd say he's having *fun*," the queen chimed in.

Ruskin shot out of the volcano, dripping with lava. His scales glowed like hot coals. Then the volcano rumbled, and a fountain of lava rose into the air and splashed back into the opening. Ruskin did a loop the loop in the fiery spray. The crowd roared with delight.

"Wow," the king remarked. "The volcano seems more active than usual."

Queen Tasha waved a fan in front of her face. "That volcano must be the cause of the heat wave we're having," she said. "What is making it so active?"

Another spout of thick molten lava burst into the air.

"Maybe the volcano is excited for the contest!" Lucas suggested.

The king frowned. "Well, let's hope it doesn't get too excited," he said, though he wasn't terribly concerned. He knew the wizards kept a watchful eye on the volcano, and most likely they had activated it for the challenge.

Ruskin returned to his seat and squawked happily.

"Crazy dragon," the prince said, shaking his head.

Meanwhile, on the edge of the arena, Clara, Gilbert, and Tublock waited for the first challenge to begin. Tublock brushed the moisture from his brow.

"It's *so* hot," he complained.

Clara's clothes felt damp and uncomfortable. She loosened her tunic to let some air flow through. "You're not kidding!" she agreed.

Gilbert harrumphed at both of them. "How we handle the heat is

most likely part of the test," he said
as if he knew everything.

Clara frowned. "And how are you
handling the heat so far?" she asked,
knowing full well Gilbert was as
uncomfortable as she was.

Gilbert wiped his brow. "Well, you
don't see *me* complaining, do you?"

Clara rolled her eyes, but she didn't dwell on Gilbert's silly behavior for long, because the mournful Horn of the Knight Spires had begun to blow again.

BALOOOOO!

The competition was about to begin.

CHAPTER 7

Three
Semifinalists

"Welcome, honored contestants!" the Head Spire called out. "The time has come for the first challenge—a test of bravery and strength." He held his hand toward the volcano. A glowing yellow dragon scale was wedged at the base of Mount Fireburst. "Whoever pulls the dragon scale out from the volcano will move on to the next round."

Clara studied the volcano and quickly spied the brilliant golden dragon scale. It sizzled and smoked with heat.

"Contestants, BEGIN!" the Head Spire called out.

A strong and giant knight in heat-protective armor and gloves marched up to the scale.

"*Psshaww,*" he scoffed. "This will be no problem for me!" He grabbed hold of the scale, and it hissed in his hands.

"OWWW!" he cried, letting go of the scale and shaking off the burn. The horn sounded, and the knight made his exit from the challenge.

One by one the contestants failed to remove the scale. Then it was Gilbert's turn. He walked toward the scale with his shoulders back and his head held high. Clara couldn't help but admire his courage.

"Go, Gilbert!" she found herself saying.

Then Gilbert laid hold of the scale, and to everyone's surprise . . . it came right out! The crowd cheered and waved their Wrenly banners.

Then it was Clara's turn, but just as she stepped forward, another squire shoved her out of the way and rushed toward the gleaming scale.

"Hey!" she shouted.

But the rude squire ignored her. He walked up and grabbed hold of the dragon scale. Then he let go instantly, screeching in pain.

Well, he got what he deserved, Clara thought. And now it was her turn. She moved toward the scale, and as she went she cleared her thoughts of anger and doubt. Then she grabbed hold of the scale.

Pop! She plucked the scale from the side of the volcano.

The crowd cheered and whistled again.

Clara examined the scale. She was surprised by how light it felt. It was also not hot at all. In fact, it was cool to the touch. She stuck the scale back into the side of the volcano and joined Gilbert in the winner's circle.

None of the other contestants after Clara succeeded in removing the scale—except Tublock. Finally the horn sounded, signaling the end of the first task.

"Hear ye! Hear ye!" the Head Spire called. "We have three semifinalists, who will continue to the next round: the squire Gilbert, the lady Clara, and the giant Tublock!"

The crowd roared. But no one cheered as loudly as Lucas.

CHAPTER 8

The Steam Caverns

The next day the three remaining contestants arrived at the base of the volcano. The Spires led them to the Steam Caverns. These were caves formed inside the volcano by ancient lava flows.

"To qualify for the final round, you must be the first through the Steam Caverns," said the Head Spire. "Good luck."

The contestants stepped into the mouth of the cave. Clara waited for her eyes to adjust to the darkness. Then she spotted three different paths—one to her left, one to her right, and one straight ahead.

"I'll take the right," Gilbert said, and darted toward that tunnel, which had the most light.

"I'll go left," Tublock said, and lumbered toward the tallest tunnel.

Clara stared at the middle tunnel.

She wasted no time and dashed into the darkness. Once inside, she had to feel her way along the cold, jagged walls with her hands. Soon the cold gave way to warmth. The farther she walked, the hotter and brighter the tunnel became. The walls around her glowed. *I must be near the heart of the volcano,* she thought. Along the way Clara brushed several spiderwebs from her face as she pressed on in the unbearable heat.

Then the tunnel narrowed. Clara started to crawl on her hands and knees along the craggy dried lava.

Hot steam burned her cheeks. Finally she squeezed through the passage and could stand up again. In the distance, she spied an opening on the other side of the volcano.

Clara gasped. The opening was guarded by a massive spider! She quickly looked for another way out.

To her right a tunnel branched away from the spider.

Clara raced through the tunnel and stopped short. There was a river of flowing lava blocking her way. A path of stepping-stones stretched across the molten river. Clara took a deep breath and hopscotched her way to the other side. She saw before her a spider-free opening ahead. The finish line was so close!

That was when Clara heard a low groan. She looked over her shoulder, and there, across the lava river, was Tublock. The giant had fallen to his knees from the heat. He wiped sweat from his brow. *This heat is too much for a giant*, Clara thought. *He'll never make it over the lava without help.*

Clara didn't think twice. She dashed back and helped Tublock to his feet. Then, step by step, Clara helped her friend across the lava. The horn sounded just as they reached the other side. Gilbert had won the challenge.

Tublock sighed and wiped a tear from his eye. "I'm sorry I slowed you down," he said.

Clara nudged him with her elbow. "I would never leave a friend alone."

The two of them walked to the finish line together. The crowd cheered as they stepped into the fresh air. Clara showed Tublock to the medical tent. Then she returned and sat down beside Gilbert.

"Congratulations on winning the challenge!" she said to him.

Gilbert bit his lip. "Thanks," he said. "That was noble of you to help Tublock."

Clara smiled as they watched the Head Spire return to the platform.

"Attention!" he shouted. "We have *two* victors in this challenge—Squire Gilbert for coming in first place and Lady Clara for never leaving a fellow competitor behind. You will both compete in the final game tomorrow."

The audience stood and clapped. Prince Lucas rushed to greet his friends.

"Congratulations to both of you!" he cried. "Tomorrow one of you may become the Thirteenth Knight!"

The Finalists

"Finalists!" called the Head Spire. "Today you must climb the stone staircase to the top of the volcano. The clue to completing the last test awaits you there."

The large crowd murmured with concern. Climbing the steep path was dangerous. Clara and Gilbert started up the stairs. Every few steps the volcano rumbled and shook.

The two contestants had to lean into the mountainside to keep from falling.

"Should we be climbing an active volcano?" asked Gilbert uncertainly.

The mountain rumbled again, and Gilbert tumbled into Clara. They held on to each other until the rumbling stopped.

"No," Clara said. "Climbing an active volcano isn't brave—it's crazy!"

Gilbert laughed nervously. "You're right," he agreed. "It's *totally* crazy."

This time they both laughed, and their laughter bonded them together.

"Maybe it would be wiser to turn back," Gilbert suggested.

The mountain shook violently again as Clara and Gilbert grabbed hold of the rocky wall.

"Or . . . what if we stuck together and helped each other to the top instead?" Clara suggested.

Gilbert admired Clara's courage and nodded slowly. "You're right."

So they both came up with a plan. First they spaced themselves apart on the stairs so they wouldn't knock each other over. Then they crouched low and used their hands to steady themselves against the side of the unstable mountain.

Slowly they crept upward. A fiery-hot wind blew down from above.

"We made it!" Gilbert said as they climbed onto a wide rim that circled the top of the smoky volcano. On the ground before them lay different weapons: A sword, a bow, arrows, potions, a spear, and the dragon scale from the challenge the day before.

Gilbert swallowed hard. "What are we supposed to do with these weapons?"

But before Clara could answer, Mount Fireburst erupted.

Clara and Gilbert covered their heads. But instead of lava, an enormous yellow dragon burst forth from the volcano. The beast flapped its great golden wings and then landed in front of the children. Gilbert picked up a sword from the ground and stood in front of Clara. The dragon raised its enormous wings and stalked toward them.

"Grab a weapon!" Gilbert cried as the dragon forced them toward the edge of the volcano.

Clara quickly grabbed the dragon scale.

"How can you fight with *that*?" Gilbert shouted. No sooner had he said it than the dragon opened its jaws and breathed a great whoosh of fire. Clara leaped in front of Gilbert and held up the scale, shielding both of them from the flame.

The two kids stood very still to see what the dragon would do next. But the dragon simply turned away and flew from the volcano. Then everything became quiet and peaceful. A gentle wind blew, and the volcano stopped shaking. The only sound they could hear was the Horn of the Knight Spires from down below.

BALOOO!

The game was over.

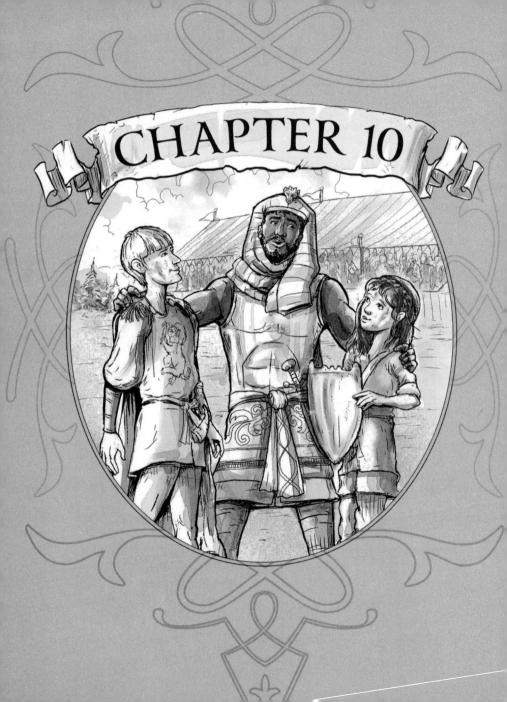

CHAPTER 10

The Thirteenth Knight

Clara and Gilbert hurried to the bottom of the volcano, sword and shield still in hand. Their faces were smudged and scorched. The crowd whistled and cheered as the two entered the arena. The Head Spire congratulated both of them. Then he lifted his hands toward the sky.

"And now the judge will select a winner!"

A great shadow swooped over the crowd, and the yellow dragon landed gracefully in front of Clara and Gilbert. The judge had arrived.

A hush fell over the crowd. The great beast stepped forward and

sniffed Clara. Then it sniffed Gilbert. The dragon stalked around the contestants in a circle. Clara noticed that the dragon had a missing scale at the base of his neck—just like the golden scale she held in her hand.

Finally the dragon bowed its mighty head to the ground . . . right in front of Clara.

"We have a WINNER!" the Head Spire cried. "Lady Clara is hereby declared the Thirteenth Knight!"

The crowd jumped to its feet and cheered. Each of the three Spires stood.

The Head Spire spoke first. "Lady Clara, by choosing the dragon scale, you showed great cleverness." He bowed and stepped back.

The second Spire stepped forward. "And by using the scale as a shield, you showed quick thinking." He bowed and stepped back.

Then the third Squire stepped forward, holding a golden sword. "By throwing yourself in front of the dragon's flame, you protected your friend. This showed great bravery." Then she handed the sword to Clara.

The crowd jumped and cheered for the new Knight Spire. They chanted, "CLARA! CLARA!"

Gilbert held out his arms and hugged Clara. "You truly deserve this honor," he said.

Then the royal family, Ruskin, Tublock, and Clara's parents came down to congratulate the winner.

"My best friend is a Knight Spire!" Lucas cried proudly.

The Head Spire patted the prince on the back and then turned to Clara. "You realize that you are the youngest Spire in history," he added. "That means you still have much training ahead of you."

Clara nodded.

King Caleb spoke up. "Clara will train right alongside Prince Lucas."

Then the Head Spire presented Clara with a suit of armor made of shimmering dragon scales. Clara curtsied, admiring the armor's unique strength and beauty.

"Thank you!" she said. "But why is the yellow dragon still bowing before me?"

The Head Spire smiled. "Because Firestorm has chosen you," he said. "From now on, she will be your partner throughout your knightly training and adventures. Just as I ride a lion and my fellow Spires ride a bear and a tiger, you will ride this dragon."

Firestorm smiled at Clara, who took the golden scale and placed it upon the dragon's neck. Instantly the Wrenly coat of arms appeared

on the scale. Then Clara put on her
new armor and climbed on top of the
beast. Firestorm stood up, spread her
wings, and lifted Clara into the sky.

The adventures of the Thirteenth
Knight had begun.

Enter
The Kingdom of Wrenly

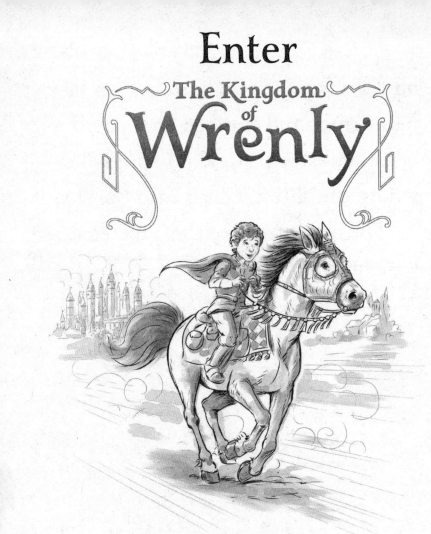

For more books, excerpts,
and activities, visit
KingdomofWrenly.com!